Sometimes My Mommy Gets Angry

"Compassionate, compelling, child wise. *Sometimes My Mommy Gets Angry* moves us into the heart of a young girl struggling to make sense of her mother's mental illness."

—NORINE G. JOHNSON, PH.D., AMERICAN PSYCHOLOGICAL ASSOCIATION
PAST PRESIDENT

"This beautiful book helps make two very important points in a way that children will understand: that mental illness does not just affect individuals, it changes families; and that support, love and understanding are crucial elements in anyone's recovery from serious illness, including mental illness."

—MARVIN SOUTHARD, DIRECTOR OF THE LOS ANGELES COUNTY
DEPARTMENT OF MENTAL HEALTH AND PRESIDENT OF
THE CALIFORNIA MENTAL HEALTH DIRECTORS ASSOCIATION

"Mental disorders are real and mental disorders are common. Bebe Moore Campbell has beautifully connected with the experience of a child living with a mentally ill parent. What a contribution!"

—DR. DAVID SATCHER, FORMER U.S. SURGEON GENERAL

"With a heartfelt story and compelling illustrations, *Sometimes My Mommy Gets Angry* helps children understand that no parents are perfect and yet still enables them to embrace the good the world has to offer."

—DAVE PELZER, AUTHOR OF *A CHILD CALLED "IT"* AND *HELP YOURSELF*

"*Sometimes My Mommy Gets Angry* is a powerful and touching story of the impact of mental illness on a child, a family and a community. This book should be a must-read for educators, therapists, community mental health workers, politicians, etc."

—HARVETTE GREY, PH.D., NATIONAL PRESIDENT 2002–2003,
ASSOCIATION OF BLACK PSYCHOLOGISTS

Sometimes My Mommy Gets Angry

BEBE MOORE CAMPBELL

ILLUSTRATED BY
E. B. LEWIS

PUFFIN BOOKS

I dedicate this book to all children whose mommies struggle with mental illness, addiction or both and pray that the village will support them—B.M.C.

To all the teachers in special education—E.B.L.

PUFFIN BOOKS
Published by the Penguin Group
Penguin Young Readers Group, 345 Hudson Street, New York, New York 10014, U.S.A.
Penguin Group (Canada), 10 Alcorn Avenue, Toronto, Ontario, Canada M4V 3B2
(a division of Pearson Penguin Canada Inc.)
Penguin Books Ltd, 80 Strand, London WC2R 0RL, England
Penguin Ireland, 25 St Stephen's Green, Dublin 2, Ireland
(a division of Penguin Books Ltd)
Penguin Group (Australia), 250 Camberwell Road, Camberwell, Victoria 3124, Australia
(a division of Pearson Australia Group Pty Ltd)
Penguin Books India Pvt Ltd, 11 Community Centre, Panchsheel Park, New Delhi - 110 017, India
Penguin Group (NZ), Cnr Airborne and Rosedale Roads, Albany, Auckland 1310, New Zealand
(a division of Pearson New Zealand Ltd)
Penguin Books (South Africa) (Pty) Ltd, 24 Sturdee Avenue, Rosebank, Johannesburg 2196, South Africa

Registered Offices: Penguin Books Ltd, 80 Strand, London WC2R 0RL, England

First published in the United States of America by G. P. Putnam's Sons,
a division of Penguin Young Readers Group, 2003
Published by Puffin Books, a division of Penguin Young Readers Group, 2005

1 3 5 7 9 10 8 6 4 2

Text copyright © Bebe Moore Campbell, 2003
Illustrations copyright © E. B. Lewis, 2003
All rights reserved

THE LIBRARY OF CONGRESS HAS CATALOGED THE PUTNAM EDITION AS FOLLOWS:
Campbell, Bebe Moore, 1950-
Sometimes my mommy gets angry / by Bebe Moore Campbell ; illustrated by E. B. Lewis
p. cm.
Summary: A little girl copes with her mother's mental illness, with the help of her grandmother and friends.
ISBN: 0-399-23972-3 (hc)
[1. Mother and child—Fiction. 2. Mental illness—Fiction. 3. African Americans—Fiction.]
I. Lewis, E. B., ill.
II. Title.
PZ7.C15079So 2003 [E]—dc21 2003001279

Puffin Books ISBN 0-14-240359-8

Manufactured in China

AUTHOR'S NOTE   This book was written to address the fears and concerns of children who have a parent who suffers from mental illness. Many forms of mental illness result in the victim experiencing extreme mood swings. A parent with bipolar disorder can have debilitating periods of depression, countered by intense manic phases. It is during the manic phase that bipolars can become enraged at the slightest provocation and often exhibit psychotic delusions. A similar tendency toward irrational anger is evident in some people who are addicted to alcohol and/or certain illegal drugs. Parents who suffer from depression and the stress of living in uncertain times may also exhibit unpredictable moods and explosive reactions to everyday situations.

Symptoms of these various mental illnesses can be managed with a combination of antipsychotic medications, mood stabilizers and psychotherapy. But because victims are often irrational, they are likely to deny that they have an illness. Noncompliance with the treatment plan is common and can last for years, with devastating consequences. Many people who have bipolar disorder self-medicate with alcohol or drugs, resulting in the dual diagnosis of mental illness and drug addiction. Some of the children being reared by a parent who suffers from some sort of mental illness may be assisted by supportive extended families; many will not.

It is my hope that this book offers children an opportunity to develop resilience by introducing or reinforcing coping strategies. It is imperative that boys and girls understand that they aren't to blame for their parents' difficulties.

The "village" that supports the children of the mentally ill—the grandparents, aunts, uncles, teachers and neighbors—can help foster within these fragile children a sense of security and hope that life can get better, and encourage self-esteem in the face of extremely trying situations.

For further information about bipolar disorder, please contact the National Alliance for the Mentally Ill at www.nami.org or (800) 950-NAMI.

When I wake up, Mommy is making pancakes. She flips them high in the air and sings, "Who wants hot, golden circles?"

"I do! I do!" I say.

Mommy raises the shade in the kitchen. "A great big yellow ball rolled in to see you, Annie." My mommy speaks very fast.

She nibbles a pancake and sips black coffee while I stuff my face. "Annie, are those golden circles yummalicious?" she asks.

"Super yummalicious!" I say.

When I finish breakfast, Mommy helps me to put on my clothes. "Beautastic!" she says when I am dressed all in purple.

She gives me a kiss and a big smile. I hope that she is still smiling when I come home. Sometimes my mommy doesn't smile at all.

Carmen and her big sister Jasmine are waiting outside
to walk with me to school. "Hey, Annie Fannie, Wannie,
Pannie, Mannie," Jasmine says. "You look cute today.
Except, what's that green stuff dripping out of your nose?"

When I reach for my nose, Jasmine laughs. "Got you good,
like I knew I would!"

In school my teacher, Mr. Perez, passes out crayons and paper. He watches my friend Kevin. "Draw something happy," he tells the class. "Kevin, take your seat!" Kevin tries to sit still, but he just can't.

Kevin draws a funny picture. He brings it over to me. "This is Trash Can Boy. He eats trash from my room so I never have to clean it," he whispers. "Trash Can Boy, eat Annie's nose!" Kevin says. I giggle.

"Kevin, go to the time-out chair," Mr. Perez says. I feel sorry for my friend.

"Excellent job, Annie," Mr. Perez says. "Tell the class what you drew."

"This is my mommy and me," I say. "We have pancakes inside us and sunshine all around us."

When I walk home, the sun is hiding. Carmen and
I fling our hair from side to side. "Oh, no," Jasmine says.
"Madam Baby Sis, three of your braids just fell on the
ground. Oooh, what's Mommy gonna say?"

When Carmen stops to look behind her,
Jasmine laughs so hard,
she almost chokes.
"I can fool ya,
because I rule ya!"
Carmen makes
a face.

"Mommy! Mommy! Come see my picture,"
I call. My neighbor Mr. Simms waves at me.
I say good-bye to my friends, but they wait
for my mommy to let me in.

"STOP ALL THAT SCREAMING," Mommy says when she opens the door. **"GET IN THIS HOUSE NOW!"** Her morning smile has disappeared like the sun.

"Hello, Judy," Mr. Simms says. "How was school today, Annie?"

"ANNIE DOESN'T HAVE TIME TO SPEAK TO YOU!" my mommy shouts.

"Judy, I didn't mean to upset you," Mr. Simms says in a quiet voice.

"YOU MIND YOUR OWN BUSINESS. YOU'RE ALWAYS SPYING ON ME," she yells.

"Mommy! Mommy! Please stop yelling," I say. But I know that she can't stop. She needs a time-out chair. I don't look at Mr. Simms or Jasmine or Carmen. I hurry inside.

I call my grandmother. "Mommy is yelling again." I begin to cry. "I wish Trash Can Boy would eat her up and bring her back when she is nice again. Why does she get so angry? She was nice this morning. I didn't do anything bad."

"No, sweetie, you didn't do anything wrong," Grandma says. "My precious Annie, you know that your mother has problems, and she hasn't gotten the help she needs. Sometimes it's hard for grown-ups to ask for help. I hope that one day she will. But your mother loves you even when she's yelling. It's okay for you to be angry. I know you love her too."

"It's not fair," I say. Every time my mommy has problems, I have to take care of myself.

"I know it's hard, sweetie," Grandma says. "You're doing a good job. I'm glad that you remember what to do when your mommy gets upset."

"I called you."

"Right. And if you feel scared?"

"I can go to Mr. and Mrs. Simms's house until you come to get me. But I don't feel scared since I'm talking to you. I can get my secret snack without bothering Mommy."

"That's right. You have raisins and peanut butter crackers, juice and pudding. Doesn't that sound good?"

"Uh-huh," I say.

"And what else can you do, Annie? Something very important."

"I can think happy thoughts," I say.

"That's right, sweetie. Maybe tomorrow your mother will feel better," says Grandma.

After I say good-bye, I hear Mommy going into her room.
I sit on the sofa and snuggle with my bear, B. B. King. I'm
Grandma's precious Annie. Mr. Perez says I do excellent
work. Tomorrow Carmen and I will have fun in school.

I eat my secret snack and read a book about
a silly cat. I take my bath,
brush my teeth
and go to bed.

In the morning it is raining. I have to be a big girl again.
I comb my hair, put on my clothes and
make my own cereal.
I try very hard.

"Hey, Curly. There's a knot in your hair," Jasmine says when I come out. She brushes my hair softly, the way Mommy does when she's not upset.

I grab the back of her skirt and stare at it. "What did you sit in?" I ask. When Jasmine starts to look, I say, "I go to school, so I can learn to fool." Carmen gives me five, and we almost fall down laughing.

"You finally got me," Jasmine says, and she is smiling.

"Our mom said it's okay for you to come to our house after school," Carmen says. She gives me a hug. Then she says to her sister, "We're so smart, we have to part!" And she grabs my hand.

"Before long, we will be gone," I say to Jasmine, who is giggling. Carmen and I run ahead.

I laugh and laugh and catch
raindrops in my mouth.

I have cereal in my tummy,
not pancakes. But I'm still full.
Sometimes my mommy has dark
clouds inside her. I can't stop the
rain from falling, but I can find
sunshine in my mind.